Tripping the Flash Fantastic

Tripping the Flash Fantastic

Allison Symes

Chapeltown Books

British Library Cataloguing in Publication Data

A Record of this Publication is available from the British Library

ISBN 978-1-910542-58-3

This edition published 2020 by Chapeltown Books
Manchester, England

CONTENTS

INTRODUCTION

I never anticipated I'd become a published flash fiction writer when I began my writing journey. I had been happily writing short stories (1500 words +) when CaféLit issued their 100 word challenge.

My first thought was you have to be kidding me? How can you tell a story in such a small word count?

My second thought was they wouldn't have issued the challenge if it was impossible. Go on, Allison, give it a go. See if you can do it.

I did and discovered it **was** possible to write stories to a tiny word count. What I didn't anticipate was how quickly I would become addicted to the form! Since then I have written across the flash fiction spectrum from five word stories right up to the top end count of 1000 words.

In this collection, you will find a mixture of word count lengths and styles. There is historical flash fiction included and some stories told in poetic form. Flash fiction is more flexible than you might think in what you can do within its structure.

I hope you enjoy this latest collection of my flash tales as much as I loved writing them.

Best wishes.

Allison Symes

TRIPPING THE LIGHT FANTASTIC

The big boss sighed as he reset the consumer unit in his kitchen.

Someone decided now was the time to trip the light fantastic. Bloody inconsiderate, he called it.

Now he had the mother of all headaches as the power went through him. It made him feel like he was a torch. Still, he would have the joy of passing on the pain.

Power always cost something and tomorrow *he* would be doing the charging.

BRINGING UP BABY

Round toys, square toys, bashed but favourite, all were strewn over the lounge. Helena suspected the substance near the top of her curtain rail was jelly. That was the price you paid for hosting your two-year-old's birthday party.

It could've been worse. In Helena's case there would never be a need to book a "magician" to entertain the kids. Magic ran in the family. When she thought of what her daughter, Amy, could do if she had enough knowledge, Helena's blood ran cold.

Not many can do that to a witch.

TIME FOR SOME PEACE

As some inconsiderate beings insisted on interfering with her peace, she must show the sods how much she hated disturbances.

She padded to the entrance. About twenty feet away were the dwarves, digging out another mine. They were wasting their time. She knew where the gold was. *She* sat on it.

Still a moment later her problems were solved. A blast of flame, no more dwarves, and she could resume guarding her baby and enjoying her rest.

It was hard work being a mother dragon.

RE-LIVING THE PAST

I don't know why you want me to go through it again. I was clear enough the first time.

I know what I said sounds incredible, but that is not the same as impossible.

Nor would I invent such a story. It seems mad. Why do you think I've spent so long hiding this?

You say you want to ensure you've got the details right. Why? You can't tell anyone! I guess it's not an easy thing to accept that you have an unusual parent but, be fair, *someone* has to be Santa. At least *you* don't have to leave out the mince pies now. We'll have them when I get back this time, yes?

LIVING A LIE

The animal crept into the cottage, ensuring he wasn't seen by anything or anyone. It was fair enough that he shouldn't be here, obvious even. But how to explain to fellow creatures he'd learned years ago how to use a human door? No. Best not go there.

Was it his fault he'd crossed some witch years ago and she'd roundly cursed him? Turned out she did more than swear at him. He caught sight of himself in the hall mirror. Ugly did not begin to cover it.

Bit ironic really. As a human he was a charming prince.

CAMPING IT UP

The tents were an amazing sight from the top of the hill. Colours ranged from virulent orange to bright blue. The richest campers had the biggest tents but that would not help.

Looking down on it all, the fairy grinned. This made a change from shoving money under pillows for spoilt human brats.

Seconds later, the spell was cast. Every tent vanished.

The fairy laughed. The humans' shouting was such a sweet sound. And it would serve his boss right for putting him on Tooth Fairy Duty. He expected it would not happen again.

THE POWER OF SUGGESTION

Show people they need something and they'll fall for it. Set your price. Don't be greedy. This is proof there's a sucker born every minute.

When told about a cache of magical objects those looking to develop their powers could use, I was on to it. Such was the power of suggestion…

The only problem was the objects were stored in a cursed box, which I touched. I'm slowly turning into porcelain. The spell has just reached my chest so I'll die soon. Nobody survives being turned into china.

There *is* a sucker born every minute. I should know.

REACHING THE END OF THE WORLD

Jeremy peered through the gateway which had a net curtain flapping in front of it.

Funny, he thought, *there is no breeze. And it looks as if I should be able to see through, but I can't. It's as if it has been deliberately veiled. Simon was right to get me to come here. He said I would have proof there is a physical end point for the world and this must be it. I wonder where that gateway leads?*

A quick, powerful shove in the back and five seconds later, Jeremy found out.

They never did find his body.

THE BACK OF BEYOND

There is not much at the back of beyond
Save loads of rubbish and a grotty pond.
Few go there. There's nothing to take to keep.
What emerges at night makes all skin creep.

JUST A MINUTE

The big mistakes don't take long to make.

Stranbarb chose the wrong shortcut and in no time he faced a witch.

Her glower told him his life could be measured in seconds. Her wand was raised and she looked as if she wanted blood. It didn't matter whose.

'Dwarf, why are you here?' She paused. 'Did you see two children go by?'

'I got lost. No.' The dwarf looked at the confectionery cottage behind the witch. Understanding dawned. He'd just prevented her from having dinner.

He looked at her again. She was smiling. She'd already selected an alternative main course.

A STITCH IN TIME

They say a stitch in time saves nine but it's no use to me. I'm a journalist. I want everything exposed.

If you obtained letters proving that your fairy monarch was offering a deal to the big bad witch, wouldn't you publish them? Especially when that witch had recently attacked a village.

I did get a choice – fifty years in jail or a transformation which carried all the risks of being eaten. What I went for will happen shortly so am scribbling now. Guess what I chose?

Croak!

THE WISH LIST

I wish I was a better person.

I wish I was not so hasty with my responses, especially when people rile me.

I wish I could undo what I have done.

I wish I did not feel so insecure. I am new here and you wouldn't believe the taunting I've experienced.

I wish I could get rid of all the bullying throughout the universes, but some would say I was the bully now.

I wish people would realise the last thing you ever do is anger a fairy godmother.

The ash pile at my feet still smoulders.

SAVING FOR A RAINY DAY

I don't want you to think I'm OCD. I'm not, honest. Mum brought me up to spend some of my money and to save the rest. I've had fun with my savings. I've had them to use when needed, but not anymore...

So yes, I believe in saving for a rainy day, though nobody has ever explained what you're supposed to do when life delivers a torrential downpour.

At first the boiler broke down. I don't know any millionaires but I am willing to bet the plumbers in this country are amongst the nouveau riche. They may ride around in white vans all day but their other car must be a Porsche. It would explain the inflated call-out charges.

Then the wretched boiler broke down again within a week. Okay the plumber sorted that out, and now, a month later, the boiler is working fine but I had to pay the call-out charge twice. And that is before my "saviour" added his labour charges and VAT.

Next, the car, my oh so reliable Mini, suddenly wasn't any more. One word to the wise: *always* sit down with a strong drink before you open your garage bill.

The wretched storm took several tiles off my roof next. I have a builder friend who did a great job putting things right. The only good thing here was that I paid money to a mate, but that's all that can be said for it.

To top it all, my poor dog, Daisy, had to go into the vets for a few days as she picked up gastroenteritis. It was touch and go for a while. I thought I was going to lose her. Did I mind paying the vets? No. It would have been heartbreaking to lose my 14-year-old collie. And she's insured so that will help.

But why must these things all come at once? My income doesn't, though it happily disappears in one go!

And now this latest bill has made me break out in a cold sweat. I had forgotten it was due but yet again I must find the money.

Why, oh why, is so much happening at once? I thought things came in threes. I must have a bad luck fairy godmother who is currently working overtime. Now how do I go about getting her sacked? Any thoughts?

A QUESTION OF BELIEF

Don't rub my nose in it, I can do that. Indeed you sometimes moan at me for doing so! I *know* I'm getting old. I can feel it in my joints. What would you have me do? Slow down? Give up? No thanks.

I'll enjoy life: the fresh air, walking, my food, and comfy bed, for as long as possible. When it's time to go I'll leave quietly, knowing I've led a good life and loved most of it.

I do wish I knew you, my beloved owner, *would* join me at Rainbow Bridge later. I do hope you will.

BEING YOURSELF

Jane Stephens suppressed the urge to scream. Of all the people to turn up in *her* library, it had to be that woman who took *her* boyfriend, Jane's Mr Wonderful. Only it seemed he was not so wonderful after all. It was *that* woman who loudly bragged about putting right the damage done by Jane. Apparently Jane had been cold. Jane grimaced. People were different, that was all there was to it.

Jane darted into a far aisle. Composing herself, she peered around the end of the horror shelves to see her nemesis heading for the "soppy" section.

The important thing, Jane told herself, *is to remember I can change how I handle this. Okay most librarians can't change their body shape but, hey, if you have the talent, use it.*

Checking nobody could see her and she was nowhere near a camera, Jane shifted slightly, muttered a few words and transformed into a snake. She slithered across and circled her nemesis's legs several times. The scream was gratifying.

By the time Jane's nemesis came back with her immediate boss, Jane was herself again.

JUDGEMENT DAY

I think I've done it this time. No more silly stuff like forgetting to put my name on my exam papers. It was a stupid thing to do. It was her fault. If I hadn't had to retrieve my notebooks at 3 a.m. because she'd thrown them out of the window again, I'd have got some sleep. I would have found it easier to concentrate then.

I hid the notebooks this time. She's not that smart. I am. I swear this will be my last visit to the exam hall.

I wish I could feel better about exams but, after three re-sits, your confidence does drop.

This time I think I am in with a chance. For once I look forward to results day, but Mother says I'm a fool. I'll show her.

Then I'm out of here. I can't wait. I only wish I could say this time would be the last one where I watched Mother down her third double vodka.

IT HAS TO BE ME

I knew it was stupid to volunteer but someone of my age had to do it. If it wasn't me, it'd be... well Her Ladyship is beautiful, funny and deserves better. If her background had been lower or mine higher, then we could've been "official". But you break customs at your peril. The "lenient" sentence is to lose a finger. You can guess what the tough sentence is, but the theory goes that people only offend once.

But now I must go to the next village, ten miles away. It will be a day's walking. The terrain is unstable and I will need breaks from the poison clouds that gather and take twenty minutes a time to disperse. Still by tonight my troubles will be over.

Why go? Our harvest failed. Our supplies are running down. If I don't go, there will be nothing and my tribe will die. It is best if only one goes and one dies. The other village, assuming I state my case well enough, will send their scapegoat to our village with a fresh supply of, not just food, but seeds. Then they too will be sacrificed.

You make your case, they sacrifice you, if all goes well (basically if there are no sudden lightning strikes), it is deemed to have pleased Fate so the request of the last sacrifice *must* be granted.

They like virgins of either sex but then who doesn't? Tough luck there. They're getting me! I hope my lover keeps her mouth shut. I wonder if she'll become... It's an odd thing to think that I might be a father already and will never know. But I won't see that sweet girl, Her Ladyship, suffer. It is best she survives.

I am writing this so that later, someone will realise it would be better if the villages forgot the past hatreds and worked together without having to kill someone from whatever village has the temerity to seek help. I'll put my notebook under this rock here and mark the stone. That should draw someone's attention. They might think it is a cry for help. It will be too bloody late. It doesn't matter how often or how loudly they call, nobody will hear me where I'm going.

WHERE THE WILD WIND BLOWS

The Witch had just finished planting out her runner beans when the farmhouse landed on her head. It'd not been a good day *before* she'd decided to do some therapeutic gardening, but her ghost recognised the day wouldn't improve now.

She stared at her red boots sticking out from under the house. Brand new they were too. What a waste. Where the hell had that bloody farmhouse come from? Flying houses weren't common in any world, even a magical one.

The Witch's ghost grimaced on spotting the girl and her dog who were also staring at the boots.

Damn, the Witch thought, *there has to be a goody-goody heroine. One, oh so squeaky clean, it makes you sick. Blast! I had a nice spell on the brew too... I could've used it on her.*

The ghost faded. Even she couldn't argue with Death, though she did try.

THE MAGICIAN

I don't know how she does it. Whatever I put down, it vanishes in seconds. I stand there, looking at her, and she looks at me knowingly. I blink, I look again, and it has all gone. She looks smug.

It must be a kind of magic. Certainly she's consistent with it. I don't know how she gets away with it though. If I tried her trick, I'd get chronic indigestion.

But then my border collie is a wizard at making her food and treats disappear.

GETTING IT RIGHT

I wish the historians would do a proper job. You would think they would record the facts. The truth is, not one has quoted me properly.

As for a certain playwright, if I still had blood in my body, it would be at constant boiling point whenever his name was mentioned. I shudder now at the thought, from anger you understand. I would have had more respect if he had admitted he was writing what you now call propaganda for his Queen and government. (I understand *that*!).

I did *not* say "My Kingdom, my Kingdom for a horse". I never did flee from battle and I was determined to live or die a King at Bosworth.

What I did say was, 'If I ever get my hands on that treacherous bastard, Stanley…'

It is funny how that never appears in the chronicles.

NOT KNOWING

You must understand that I was brought up to do my duty. It comes above everything. *Everything* I tell you. I do not know what happened to my brothers. I know what I believe happened, but have no proof. It is safest to say that I think the official verdict is open to question. A lot of questions. One day someone will ask them.

One day *all* members of my family will be buried properly and with honour. What happened to him after Bosworth was horrific. Nobody should ill-treat the bodies of the vanquished and even more so of an anointed king.

My fiancé says that was not a command of his. In the heat of the moment behaviours of "lesser" people can lapse, and it could just as easily have happened to him. That is true. He owes so much to Lord Stanley.

He also says it happened so quickly, there was no time for a proper burial and it is best forgotten now.

Yes, it probably is. No good can come out of asking awkward questions after the event. It is not as if I could change anything. There have been dark forces at work and even I would not be safe. I must focus on now. I cannot help my brothers but I can help my sisters. They will marry well. I will see to that. My fiancé has seen it is the best thing to do. It rewards his most important followers and brings our two royal houses closer together.

So I am working to unite the realm. I will lead the way with my marriage. There must be no more war. I am saddened at how much damage has been done. I hope my children will have the bright and prosperous future my brothers had stolen from them. That would give me some consolation.

I am Elizabeth of York, shortly to be Henry Tudor's Queen. Pray for me. Nobody knows who I light candles for when I am in church. My uncle will know.

GOOD TO GO

He looked at himself in the mirror. It was no good. He couldn't put it off any longer. The duty called. Still he had the very best in transport and food and drink supplies were generous. The only problem with that was answering the call of nature, but that was his problem and he'd deal with it.

He looked at the clock. Yes, time to be off. Rudolph and the others would be waiting.

If Santa prided himself on anything, it was his punctuality.

THE RECRUIT

'*Can* Jim do this? He stares into space.'

'Have you shown him what to do?'

'A million times, boss.'

'*Really?* You know my powers mean I can detect exaggeration from a mile away.'

The elf bowed. 'Sorry, Santa, but we're rushed off our feet, we need workers but if Jim can't…'

'Perhaps he's scared. You remember *your* first Christmas here?'

The elf blushed. 'Breaking the tree baubles *was* an accident, sir.'

'Quite. *He* didn't mean to knock that wretched tree over. We must move it. See to it, and then send Jim to me. It's time for an encouraging word. You improved no end after you had yours!'

TIME TO BE OFF

'We don't usually leave the sheep, boss. You say it's dangerous.'

'Yes, lad, but this is different.' The head shepherd gazed at the youngest herdsman.

'The wolves and other predators are still out there, boss.'

'Our visitors will make sure our animals are all right while we visit Bethlehem, lad.'

'They didn't *say* so, boss. They just talked and sang about "Glory to God".'

'True, lad, but they know we need our sheep. Come on, let's go. Are you nervous? Is that why you're dilly dallying?'

The young herdsman gulped. 'Be fair, boss, it's not every day you meet the Son of God.'

~~~~~

Author's Note: The next story is my response to a writing prompt challenge I set during the cyberlaunch of my debut flash fiction collection, *From Light to Dark and Back Again* (also available from Chapeltown Books). The launch was huge fun – and I'm delighted to get another story from it for this collection!

THE TERRIFIED DRAGON

The dragon was surrounded by angry humans with weapons and realised to his dismay he was supposed to blast them all away.

One thing that wretched witch who cursed him had done was enable him to keep his speech, and she had told him it was only his pleading that made her concede. The sight of someone grovelling always made her laugh especially if they were male. Speech would finally be useful, the way he hoped one day it would be. Maybe he could make these humans understand.

'I didn't steal your meat, I don't see how you can accuse me of that,' the dragon cried. 'I can easily get my own. I don't like human meat. You're sinewy.'

The nearest human, a thin elderly man (who the dragon realised would taste revolting), sneered. 'Really?'

'Yes, really, and just how many talking dragons have you met?'

The crowd fell silent. It was a relief to the dragon not to hear their curses. The language was dreadful – and that was just from the kids.

'I haven't always been a dragon. I was cursed by a witch. I destroyed her garden. I did it for a laugh. And to return that laugh, she turned me into this. I have been hunted everywhere I go. I avoid you lot. You are nothing but trouble.'

The crowd began muttering again but a middle-aged man, looking thoughtful, raised his hand. Silence fell. The man wore a striped apron and the dragon didn't want to know what the red stains were (he guessed) or where they came from.

The man cleared his throat. 'We are always having trouble with the Xibians raiding our supplies, right? We have no effective way of stopping them! We have one now.' He gave the dragon a hard stare. 'We could do a deal with this guy. He guards us. In return we share our meat with him. He cooks it for us too. You know what trouble we have getting our barbecues to light properly. There's that problem solved too. What do you say?'

BYPASSING THE SYSTEM

No matter what he did, the magic wouldn't work. His pronunciation was perfect. He'd won prizes for his wand waving. But here he was surrounded by spell books and other magical materials and not one thing was making even the slightest spark. Any hope of achieving anything useful was rapidly heading down the pan.

The world weary face on the crystal ball grimaced. The youngsters all tried this the moment they'd learned enough magic and the teachers were in an Ofmage meeting. Nobody succeeded.

Still this latest farce had gone on long enough.

'Give it up, boy. Nobody gets a fortune out of the National Lottery by magic. Go and get a ticket like everyone else does.'

LOSING MYSELF

8th August 1999

Graxia, for heaven's sake reconsider your magical career. Your lineage shouldn't endanger you because the Queen offends our entire world by importing her human paramours. If she ruled decently, she wouldn't have problems. You know you're a decent fairy. Our world needs more like you.

I've kept moving due to the one person, who knew what I did at Red Hill, pursuing me. It *wasn't* a ploy to cause you trouble honestly.

By the time you get this, the Council should've tackled your troublesome aunt. A dragon will be involved. I hear the bell. I'm not expecting anyone. Damn. It's her. Time to fly…

29th March 2003

Graxia, it is one hell of a gap since I wrote but I've spent more time in ditches than I care to relate. I finally bought a cottage only for a hurricane to destroy it. Had I been cursed? I found no traces. Trust me, I looked.

What do you remember about me? The eccentric wildlife obsessed fairy out in all weathers? The best escape was to lose myself in a new persona, that of the old biddy lecturing everyone on the environment…

Had folk known I defeated Mestrinna, the legendary Chief Witch (the best witch leader ever), at Red Hill, I'd never have been left alone. I've no time for the celebrity fairy circuit or miffed witches!

Mestrinna wanted to recruit me. I kept refusing, so she arranged for the residents of Red Hill to force me into showing my skills. It wasn't the first time she used what Earth would call human shields. I should've fled, but I couldn't leave those poor villagers to their fate, so I exposed my magic. I hid but Mestrinna laughed and said, "Got you!" and threatened to use the detonation spell, meaning the end of us all within a radius of three miles, if I didn't join her immediately. So I fought Mestrinna and won.

Your aunt would've ensured I fought for her if she realised who "that heroic fairy" was. What did she do to other "useful" fairy godmothers? Send them out to fight fiends at all times and was she sympathetic when they returned injured? What do you think?

I ran…

I see a shadow. Bloody hell, how can she know I'm here?

5th October 2005

Graxia, to say my life would be ruined if my pursuer catches me is an understatement. I'm 350 years old. I've spent 300 years on the run. It's felt twice as long.

I thought when your aunt was eaten head first by that dragon, my problems were over. I thought Mestrinna would calm down (no more provocation). You've restrained Mestrinna well since I've been "gone". I've watched. Now you're Queen… chosen by the Council… just remember they selected the dragon.

I knew I'd have to lose myself directly after Red Hill. Now it's second nature but it wasn't at the start. Suppressing magic isn't easy. When your aunt was alive, avoiding situations where you had to use magic was easier said than done. I did it. Gained a reputation for cowardice. I ran at any hint of trouble to "save the wildlife". Did I care? To begin with, yes. I was no coward at Red Hill.

Then I realised the taunting helped. Mestrinna knew she faced no coward. This coward being mocked couldn't be her nemesis then. With your aunt gone, I only had to fool Mestrinna. That should've been easy. Ha!

6th October 2005 – 1 pm

Wow! These are my first consecutive diary entries. Mestrinna is pursuing me. Call her off. I've seen her towering black hat. Nothing stops me from being my own fairy, including you. Damn… there's something on the roof…

6th October 2005 – 3 pm

Graxia, the disruption was next door's cat. It *was* a cat. I know when a magical being changes species.

The wretched Fairy News Network reveals you've taken to the magical life, with its danger, and the Crown, with its pomp. Do I regret my actions? No. You accelerated through the ranks thanks to my "not being available".

Call off Mestrinna. Only you can. Your aunt put expertise above royal blood so you wouldn't automatically have got promotion. It was no coincidence the reward posters seeking the Red Hill heroine were never answered. I destroyed loads!

11th October 2005

It seems I might stay here. I've planted daffodils for next year. Are you thinking I haven't got lost given the pursuit? You're wrong. Bar Mestrinna, the Kingdom hasn't a clue.

I thought I'd never worry about Mestrinna again. Always ensure nothing from your past can haunt you. Mestrinna officially skulked in her castle but only I realised she sneaked out to see if this wildlife nut was the fairy who nearly killed her. This diary will reach you once I'm dead. Some magic-proof charms have ensured that. If Mestrinna could use you to get to me, she would.

12th October 2005

A thought occurs, something I should've considered before. If I'd fulfilled my fairy godmother role, the pressure would've been off you all these years, yes? Remember you faced up to Mestrinna. That's made you. Damn. Someone's walked through the wall.

Postscript by Mestrinna

Darling, Graxia (ha!), or should I say Ma'am, I just missed you last week! Gave you and the Council a fright, didn't I? I found this book on the sofa in this tatty cottage. "Fairy Rose" vanished as I walked through her wall. She always loved that spell.

I've known for ages that wildlife mad biddy nearly killed me at Red Hill. There are things no magic disguises.

I wasn't going to kill someone who nearly defeated me, funnily enough. Your aunt would've recruited her too.

At least you're not upsetting the realm. You'll do as monarch. You'll get no higher praise.

I'm getting Rose. She'll contact you again later. She won't be able to help herself. Her diary shows a desperate need to confess! Nobody keeps losing me. Correction. Rose has. I swear she's not getting away with it.

Graxia, don't block me. Who do you think told your Council where to get that dragon?

THE SILENCE

It was the perfect way to shut up Mr Know-it-all. The only surprise was not having thought of it before, but perhaps she hadn't been provoked enough. Not a problem now though!

Making her special sticky toffee pudding meant she could enjoy the silence for hours. He never could resist it. And she had finally glued his mouth shut.

When he woke up he'd be none the wiser. If anything he'd blame the pudding for sending him to sleep early, a good meal often had that effect on him, and the copious amounts of alcohol disguised the taste of the extra special ingredient.

THE PAST – READY OR NOT?

She could guarantee a ruined career if her past came out. Her life would become a nightmare. Her old work wasn't something that could be explained away or laughed off. But she'd known there would be a price to pay for daring to be different and it could've been worse. Fatally worse.

At least she'd come to Earth at the right time to make a new quieter life. They had stopped the witch hunts at least. She loved her new job. It was her life now.

But she wasn't using her fairy godmother skills to speed up the parcel deliveries at the Sorting Office, even at Christmas when the extra assistance would probably be appreciated.

It would still be cheating. And given that was why she was thrown out of her old world, she wasn't making the same mistake again.

MENU CHOICES

Humpty Dumpty sat on a wall
He went down in history for it.
Humpty Dumpty had a great fall.
The King's men said no to omelette
And instead had our hero poached.

KEEPING QUIET

Jenny felt it best to keep the portal to the magical world quiet
Or there would be no end of trouble, maybe even a riot.
What human could resist the urge to steal the strange power
Not known on Earth and then use it until it went sour,
As all magical power does when abused?

Jenny sighed. She knew her own kind too well.
Getting magical power would be its own form of hell.
So she must act for mankind's greater good,
Though they'd never know and she really should
Cast her spell so anyone near the portal became confused.

A confused human will not meddle with what they don't know
But interfering directly could cost Jenny dearly, so,
Best the deed was done quietly and discreetly
She'd tie up loose ends so everything finished neatly.
Meaning Jenny would not face being accused

Of meddling in magical affairs – Jenny knew the short fuse
Of the Fairy Queen could undo Jenny's ruse
To save her fellow humans from what she wished.
Would go away, never exist, so nothing could be dished
Up on a hybrid girl trying to avoid being misused.

Oh there'd been talk of using Jenny to test out new spells.
It would save pure blood fairy folk from all kind of hells
Given it was not unknown for charms to go horribly wrong.
Well, Jenny wasn't joining in with that particular song.
She would keep magic out of her life, she would not be bruised.

The portal had not been there yesterday, that Jenny did know.
It didn't take much to make her suspicions grow.
The Fairy Queen was trying to draw Jenny in,
This was one fight Her Majesty would not win.
Jenny's blood was her own; it was not going to be used

As some kind of horrid test for new magical ways,
They could find their own scapegoats for their strange ways.
Jenny was better off out of it and so she would be,
The Queen would be angry but she would also see
Jenny's attitude to magic was where she refused

To be used as anyone's puppet or prop and so evade
Strange peoples, odd powers, things that all bade
Jenny to do what they wanted with no thought of her.
Well, sod that, Jenny thought, I will not stir
From my home planet – I am not amused

At what my dear mother has landed me in, by
Leaving her world somewhere up in that sky.
And coming here because she wanted a new life
To be a mere human, and the dearly loved wife
Of Jenny's father who did not know of the ruse.

Jenny sighed. Life was complicated enough
Without rogue beings making it very tough.
Well, the portal was sealed up now and would not budge
Jenny had come up with a useful and irrevocable fudge.
Her fears of the magical world were over, she mused.

No way were they coming here, Jenny thought, well not again.
Now they will stay put in their world and not be a pain
To any mere human, given they look down on us all.
They stay in their realm if they want a ball.
I will not let the chains of this portal ever be loosed.

WHAT THE NEIGHBOURS THINK

Had the neighbours seen the appearance of a witch in the huge chestnut tree? Mary fervently hoped not. She also hoped they hadn't seen her frantically wave at the witch indicating exactly where she could go. Back into the sky on that dodgy looking broomstick and away from her.

What is it about me that attracts the oddballs? Mary poured a cup of tea and added a decent amount of brandy to it. Even by her standards, the appearance of a witch was unusual. Annoyingly it was nowhere near Halloween so Mary couldn't pretend it was one of the neighbourhood kids taking a prank that bit too far.

Looking again out of her kitchen window, Mary sighed with relief. The witch had gone. She turned back to her tea only to discover she now had company in her kitchen.

'Aren't you going to make *me* a cup of tea then, sister?'

Mary grimaced. She now knew where the witch was.

SEEING IS BELIEVING

When Ben was unwell, strange signs appeared in the sky above his house. For one thing, the sky would change colour depending on just how ill he was – yellow, appropriately for when he was sick, blue for when he had a cold, and a virulent pink when he was running a fever.

How anyone in the area missed seeing that, he had no idea. He just wished the sky would stay the normal colour it was supposed to be. Even one sneeze made him nervous now.

He still had no idea whether he was cursed or if it was the property itself. The previous owner claimed a former fairy godmother lived at the place and there was "left over" magic making the house protective of its owner.

Ben had laughed. He'd bought the place because it was convenient: by the railway station for commuting, near enough to the country for walking to be a pleasure at weekends, and within ten minutes' drive in any direction to his family and friends.

Now Ben didn't laugh, though he did joke the strange signs off with the postman. It was the only way to turn his postman's attention away from the huge Leylandii hedge in the front garden that decided it was going to stop Ben having any visitors by swallowing the poor guy whole.

Ben's intervention by standing in front of the Leylandii made the hedge stop, as if rooted to the spot (*which it damn well should've been*).

It was just a pity Ben hadn't been able to save the milkman earlier that month when Ben had shingles. Still once bitten, twice shy. Ben vowed that bloody hedge would get nobody else. If only he had the nerve to take the hedge trimmer to it…

IDENTITY

Walter was sure he'd seen the new postman on a Wanted poster. That rough stubble, the shape of the face, that warty nose – yes, he was recognisable from it, put up near the Post Office only yesterday. Walter glared at the man on his doorstep, not sure what else he should do. At 85, Walter was going to think more than twice about being a hero. And this stranger looked like he worked out at the gym several times a day.

'And what do you want?' Walter wasn't apologising for being grumpy. He wasn't used to visitors on his doorstep at 7.30 a.m., let alone ones that looked like criminals. *Maybe it's me*, Walter reflected, *but all young men look like criminals these days.*

'I didn't mean to disturb you, sir, but there is smoke coming out of your kitchen window,' the young man pointed to Walter's left.

'Oh bugger, I left the bacon on,' Walter turned to go back into the house but the young man clamped his wrist.

'I wouldn't if I were you, sir. I can see flames now. You'd best come out here. I've called the Fire Brigade.'

Walter looked at his kitchen but felt himself being tugged out of the door. The guy who looked like a criminal had a decent grip on him and Walter felt it best not to argue.

'You don't think I'll need to go into a home?' Walter asked. 'I've never left the bacon on before.'

'It was an accident,' the young man replied. 'Could've happened to any of us, but you could have a chat with your doc if you're worried.'

Walter nodded and then watched the fire engine race up to his front gate.

It was as the Fire Brigade were finally extinguishing the flames, Walter found out his saviour was called Steven, aged 33, married with one son, and was an off duty copper, who'd arrested the guy on the poster late last night.

Walter still didn't like the stubble though.

CHOICES

I ran 'til I could run no more,
I dropped to the thick forest floor.
The sounds behind me had now gone
But I knew it was a big con.
They weren't fooling me anymore.

I guess it would've helped if I had
Chosen not to turn to the bad.
But when a girl's luck is so down
And she can nick a pretty crown
To not do so would just seem mad.

Who would miss that one little piece?
Not the king. Not even his niece,
And she was the one who wore it!
No, I thought, I do need a bit
Of luck my way, with bad to cease.

I'd sell this lovely work of art.
I knew I must make myself part
With it so I could try to use
The money to feed my own muse.
Well, all writers need a good start!

MISHAPS

Going back in time had its drawbacks. For one thing, it could be tricky working out what era he'd reached. The way people dressed didn't always provide enough information. Medieval costume in England covered hundreds of years for a start. It could also be tricky keeping up with what reign you were now in and this was crucial. Get that wrong and you could be jailed or worse.

The time traveller shuddered as he recalled how narrowly he'd escaped execution in King John's era for innocently enquiring what King Richard was up to these days just outside the gates of Nottingham Castle. It was the kind of thing that could happen to any hapless time traveller around the universes. All *he* knew was it wasn't going to happen to him again. He had to find a way of accurately measuring his time.

And the clock the salesman had sworn kept accurate time did anything but! The time traveller had throttled the fake cuckoo in it millennia ago, as it refused to stop its racket and he couldn't be bothered to simply fix the mechanism.

So where was he now? Peering outside of his time machine, which conveniently turned itself into a post-box, all the time traveller saw was the face of a woman who was about to shove letters into his "slot". One look into his staring green eyes and she screamed and passed out. He flicked a switch on his machine. Time to move on again then.

JUMPING TIME

Going forward in time had its drawbacks. It would help if the known universes had a standard unit of time but that would make life too easy.

The time traveller sighed. His controls showed he was on Earth, which was good. At least there'd be oxygen, water, and, if he was lucky, a decent café. He could demolish some bacon and chip butties right now.

Time travel took its toll on the body from giving him a ravenous appetite to removing his clothing without warning.

He swore it was his machine having a laugh at him but had no idea how to rectify it. He flew. He wasn't technical.

And he wasn't fussy over cuisine. As long as it was cheap and cheerful, it was fair game, though he once was beaten by an enraged old lady when he thought the "cheap" bit referred to her budgie.

So where was he now and, more importantly, when?

The costumes of the humans he could see out of his time machine's main window were brightly coloured and 'vivid' was far too tame a term to use.

Damn! That told him nothing. There was nothing for it. He'd have to ask.

He stepped out of his ship, which he noted now resembled a scarlet hot air balloon.

What with the post-box earlier, his machine clearly had a thing for shades of red today.

The noise made him turn to see dozens of women pointing at him. They were laughing.

He looked down. He was naked. He fled into his ship.

Why the hell had they laughed?

DECISIONS

He could watch the world end or jump on to the alien spaceship that encouraged visitors. All dreams of girls, breaking into show business, hell, even getting one win on the Premium Bonds ended now, but he'd live. He jumped. To his surprise, he was applauded.

'The monkey has talent.'

He turned to see where the voice came from. He saw a red biped about eight foot tall. Behind was a group of smaller red bipeds. All wore black tunics which covered them bar their square heads, which reminded him of blank television screens. They even had a single antenna in the middle of their heads. He wondered if they could get the movie channel.

'I'm not a monkey. My name is Jeff. I am human.'

'It talks, master,' one of the smaller bipeds nearest the big one said. 'What else does it do?'

The thing hit Jeff on the head.

Jeff swore. The biped hit him again. Jeff swore again.

'Primitive reaction,' the master said. 'Dump this one. Get another. Take him to the execution chamber.'

Jeff began tap dancing. If they wanted skills they could have them.

The master held up a clawed hand. 'We keep this one. Take him to the kitchens. He'll need feeding. We've got guests after dinner. We need something for a show.'

Jeff sighed. Of all the ways to break into the entertainment industry…

VEGETABLES ARE GOOD FOR YOU

He should have realised the significance of the garlic ban in this Transylvanian town. But, as the vampire bit, he realised it was too late to worry about it now.

How odd it was that it was his mother's oft-repeated phrase – he should eat his greens as vegetables were good for him – should reverberate in his mind as he lost consciousness.

Of all the thoughts to go into the next world with, he'd never anticipated it would be this one.

TIME IS FOR OTHERS TO WORRY ABOUT

When it came to being late, there was nobody to match him. Whether it was going for the bus to college and then later work, he could guarantee his timekeeping would be out by minutes, more than enough time to miss any public transport going. It was okay for them to be late but not him.

Fortunately his mother had drilled it into him to always go for the bus *before* the one he actually needed, else he knew he'd never have stayed in employment for long. People get fed up with others being continually late.

When he left home, he swore it would be different. He had tried setting all the clocks in his house five minutes fast but soon realised it wouldn't work as he defaulted to what he knew was the correct time. And when it came to getting married, he got to the aisle barely a minute ahead of his bride.

Still, on the plus side, he *was* late for his own funeral.

HABITS

She started, suddenly realising this was her 15th armed robbery of the year. And it was only mid-January so she still had some time to beat her own record of 38. She wasn't fazed by the law or by cameras. Neither was she concerned about those she robbed. All she knew was she needed the thrill of planning the raid, carrying it out, and getting away with it.

Her addiction was getting worse. What had started as a minor amusement was now something she couldn't do without. It wasn't for the money or goods obtained. Sometimes she only took a tiny amount. It was the being able to do it undetected that she lived for.

But then it helped when you were a trainee witch and your specialist spell was invisibility. All anyone ever saw on those wretched cameras that were everywhere these days were goods being "lifted" without any sign of the person doing the lifting.

That was how she liked it.

EVERYONE HAS TO HAVE A HERO

She thought she could claim the world's unluckiest cook title and win it, no questions asked. She did burn toast, baked beans, anything else that could go on a hob or into an oven. The jokes hurt. They were also repetitive. She did try to concentrate. She did set an alarm but somehow things still went wrong. Just because she burned things, that didn't mean she was stupid, but it was a pity others didn't see that.

Even when she took up history as an OU course, the mockery for her cooking continued. It seemed if you were bad at one thing, you had to be bad at them all. Still she loved her studies and, in the process, discovered a hero, who was a man who loved books, literature, *and* burnt the cakes. If only she'd been able to meet him...

It was a pity King Alfred had been born so many centuries before her!

UNDERSTANDING

I'm a time travelling alien. I make myself look like whatever species I'm going to visit and blend in well. You just need to know the physiology of the world you're going to and the rest you pick up as you go along. Books can be helpful too.

Despite the hassles of time travel (you can become terribly sick if you move in time too fast), it also has its fascinating side. I've lived alongside some of your most famous historical figures at crucial moments in their lives and really got to understand them. I love character study. Sometimes I can get to share what I know with others, as I am now.

She never knew what I was. She just knew I was different. But so was she, especially for her era. You were right to call her "great". She truly was. We became friends, as much as her rank would allow. It helped that I never married. She never did. I understood why she didn't. I could never tell her why I didn't; I fled from my planet's arrangements for that. Let's just say they're not gentle. The funny thing is, I think she would've understood but I didn't dare risk it.

I saw the tension she lived under for most of her adult life. Always at risk of being murdered (simply because of who she was born to when all is said and done, and later her faith was deemed by some as "wrong" – are they good reasons to kill someone? I think not).

She was forced to put people to death, you know. How often can you save someone from the block when your own Parliament is baying for their blood and when the person concerned has been complicit in wanting you dead for years?

She genuinely was distraught when the Scottish woman was put to death. It wasn't playacting.

An anointed Queen putting another to death? Of course Elizabeth was going to be upset. She had been through it before, you know. People forget that.

She saw herself as being in the role of her father. While she welcomed that as part of being a monarch, she didn't welcome it for this.

She was grieving for the Queen when Mary was put to death.

She was grieving for her mother.

Anne Boleyn.

MY GIRL

I hope my little girl will be well. I have had promises from people that they will take care of her, but will these hold? He is so powerful. But even if he wouldn't want to harm her, would he if political circumstances demanded it? He did acknowledge her as his. It is the only comfort I can take with me.

There is nothing I can do now but pray. My ladies think I am in prayer for myself. I'm not. I'm praying for her. That she will survive, do well in life, and not allow the fact that I'm her mother to ever get in her way.

I know how hated I've been but I did love him. I still do, despite what he is going to do tomorrow. He thinks I failed him. He failed me but you cannot tell him that. I think, later, he will realise how I loved him. I can't see any other woman doing what I did. Oh they'll fall in with his wishes. One may even give him his precious male heir but I gave him my intelligence, my wit, my all, and a beautiful little girl who inherited everything. She could do great things. I pray she does.

Tomorrow is 19th May 1536. I will go to my death bravely. I know how I die will be reported to her later when she is old enough. I want her to be proud of me.

I shouldn't have been so nasty to Catherine or Mary. I regret that now. I know now how it is to love someone so passionately you would do almost anything for them. Catherine was trying to protect Mary. I've done what I can for Elizabeth. I hope it is enough.

I could've gone abroad quietly with her but my loyalty is to her and to England, not to him. England will need her. I just hope the damage done to Mary does not impact on the country. She is a troubled soul and I contributed to that. I shouldn't have been such a bitch. I wish I could tell her. Maybe somewhere up there, Catherine will know, given she has gone on before me. She'd be horrified at what Henry is doing. I couldn't see her wanting Elizabeth to suffer. Catherine would have shipped Elizabeth and I off somewhere quietly I think.

But England will need Elizabeth. I just know it deep in my soul. And when my soul goes to be with God tomorrow, my last prayers will be for her to serve God and her country well, as nothing else matters – and certainly not men. I hope something of that gets through to her.

THE HELP

He'd never do it all by himself, you know. It was my idea that he should check the list twice. We already know who's naughty and nice you see, but it makes him feel better and that's no bad thing. The world will never be ready for a depressed Santa.

Depressed? Yes. Between you and me he's not keen on sherry and would rather eat Rudolph's carrots than yet another mince pie. Be honest, you've seen one mince pie, you've seen them all. But the poor soul can hardly say so.

If there's any chance of you lot putting out the odd cookie, slice of Christmas cake, anything to ring the changes, that would be great. I still think it's a miracle he hasn't developed diabetes but there you go.

Now I must be off. The great man has just put on the red suit. We'll be off shortly. And he must never know I spoke to you.

A CHRISTMAS MESSAGE

It is the way at this time of year
To spread some words of seasonal cheer.
It is time for me to have my go
Without aping Santa's "Ho, Ho, Ho".
Merry Christmas and Happy New Year!

THE GUILTY SECRET

I stumbled through the woods.
Not sure what was following me.
I knew I had to dump the goods
No other eye should ever see.

I DISLIKE MONDAYS

Monday's child is fair of face
The rest of the week is a disgrace.
Monday's child is oh so wise.
They never forget to moisturise!

AND THEN THERE ARE TUESDAYS...

Tuesday's child is full of grace
When they said, I pulled a face.
You'd be graceful, would you not
When a good life is your lot.
And you know Wednesday's brat doesn't have your luck
Facing a day full of woe and life's muck.

HOW TO OVERCOME SPIDER WOE

Miss Muppet wasn't getting caught out a second time. Oh dearie me, no.

She wrapped up warm, took supplies and went where she knew no spider would ever go.

The Antarctic!

Whether she'll come back though is another matter.

SAYING GOODBYE

I knew the time would come but I still wasn't ready. I kept it together, somehow kept my nerves steady. I have no idea how.

It would be best if others fell apart. Do I really need to show the world *my* broken heart?

ENOUGH IS ENOUGH

She knew she had to stop it. It wasn't doing her any good and any comfort she derived from it had vanished long ago.

She put on her huge black coat, it made her look slim, grabbed her cavernous bag and shook out the massive pork pie she had stored in there since coming home last night. She grimaced at it, picked it up and, as she left her flat and walked out of the roadway, she dumped the pie in the community bin.

Today she would start again. Enough was enough. She took a deep breath and headed to where she knew the slimming group met. She'd put off going for ages. But today was different.

She was not going to be mistaken for a giant tomato on legs again by anyone. She would show the world she could do it. And when she had, she would get the most rotten tomatoes she could find, hide and hurl the things at those people who'd humiliated her tonight. She knew where they were. They did not know where she was. And it would stay that way.

A year later, the local papers appealed for help in tracking a mystery assailant going around pelting rotten veg at people coming off the number 28 bus at different times.

She laughed.

THE PINK ROSE

The lady didn't remember the pink rose or when it was given to her.

Her daughter did though.

The lady couldn't remember who made sure she could always see the pink rose, no matter what position they put her in as they fought the constant battle against pressure sores. All she knew was the rose was pretty and it was soothing to see it.

All the daughter knew was *the lady* couldn't fight her own battles anymore. So the daughter would do all that was possible to fight those battles for the lady.

The lady couldn't remember teaching the daughter to read when she was little.

The daughter didn't either, just knew she was grateful for it.

And when the Alzheimer's finally got the lady, the daughter took the pink rose home and placed it on her writing desk.

She does remember and fears for the time when she may not.

The pink rose will be her remembrance and a warning to her as her love for stories continues as she writes her own.

THE WORKING MAN

In the middle of the Christmas rush
There was an old man carving a brush.
He was clearly an expert in wood,
He could make any timber look good.
Right by the old High Street church he was,
He so wanted to be there because
The God he loved was a carpenter
A worker should be at the centre
Of the scene, as the shepherds had been
There long before the wise men were seen.
The man liked a God who worked with His hands
In the tableau He was in swaddling bands.

A DAY OUT

Jamie slammed the front door. He must feed the Resington giant ducks. It was like jury duty – everyone had a go.

Finally it was his turn. Still nobody said he had to rush to the lakes. So he wasn't going to do so.

Jamie felt that the giant ducks on Earth Mark 2 sought revenge for all the duck a l'orange consumed on Earth Mark 1. Last week the news revealed that the ducks had raided a now-deceased shopper and did terrible things with her Paxo.

At the oval-shaped lake, Jamie hoped the ducks would look friendlier after eating their meat.

THE CAKE BAKE

A wave of the wand saw the job done.
The smiling godmother disappeared.
Her client, who couldn't bake buns,
Would now make the cake of the year.
Whatever tins Rachel did choose
Would turn her into the perfect cook
With all to gain and nothing to lose,
More success in the fairy's book.

Rachel put the mix from the blender
Into her loaf tin, hoping this time,
This cake would be tasty and tender
She hated her pals' rock-like mime.
'Don't worry,' said the cake with a sigh,
'Your many baking accidents
Would make any baker howl and cry
We *will* sort out your confidence.'

The fruitcake was baked and, once cool,
Rachel brushed it with some melted jam.
Confidence boosted, no more a fool,
On went the marzipan and then wham!

Came the icing, (ready to roll kind),
The cake said loudly, 'Jolly well done.'
But Rachel was unhappy to find
Baking judging itself being done!

The cake was dressed and ready to go,
'Yes,' said its loaf tin, 'down someone's mouth.
They'll eat you quick or they'll eat you slow
You're going inside, you're going south.'
Rachel frowned on hearing the loaf tin talk,
It was bad enough hearing the cake speak!
Rachel cries, the fairy breaks a walk
To say, 'stop fretting, magic won't leak.'

When the cake cried out, Rachel despaired
Would it talk at her very special do?
Could spells be cancelled or just repaired?
What damage would removing this brew do?
Justice takes so many forms though.
The cake showed fear on seeing the knife.
The cake berated Rachel for its woe.
'The loaf tin was right, I end my life.'

The cake's remains ensured Rachel heard
Its frank views on kids and all their stains.
Did she see where they shoved lemon curd?
It just confirmed kids were right pains!
Parties were for adults who ate well
Who didn't bolt, or were fiends from hell.
Rachel's only response was to sigh.
Magic made a cake talk, why, just why.

She called the fairy to stop the spell.
As in *The Sorcerer's Apprentice*.
Rachel told the fairy things were hell.
Now it was time for the momentous.
It was time for things to be put right
The fairy scoffed all the cake's remains.
It was one way to tackle the blight.
And had one bonus – no cake stains!

'Spell dealt with, dear, let's keep this quiet.
I've never seen you so full of pain.
I'll tell all you've gone on a diet
And that is all that you'll gain.

Colleagues won't know I cancelled my spell.'
Rachel smiles, 'I know I won't bake well.
Let's say goodbye to this sad affair.
Magic has its place. Please send it elsewhere!'

THE JOYS OF THE WRITING LIFE

When everything is said and done
This writing lark is such fun,
But what nobody then tells you
Is that it can be hell too.

Characters won't leave you alone.
You cut word counts to the bone.
You're never sure a piece is done
Though acceptance proves you've "won".

But something drives you on to write,
Work hard and get your piece right
As much as it could ever be.
You have to prove yourself, see.

OTHER COLLECTIONS BY ALLISON SYMES

From Light to Dark and Back Again

This is a collection of flash fiction pieces. The tones vary from humorous to dark and back again but all reflect Allison's style of fiction. Some have appeared on Cafélit (http://cafelit.co.uk) and others on Shortbread Short Stories. The latter are some of the very first pieces she wrote years ago, Cafélit is more recent and other stories are brand new for this collection.

"A wonderful collection of light and dark stories, short enough to entice one to read when time is limited but long enough to be enjoyable. Allison Symes has cleverly combined light and dark stories which kept me guessing as to how they would end." (*Amazon*).

Order from Amazon:

ISBN: 978-1-910542-06-4 (paperback)

978-1-910542-07-1 (ebook)

Chapeltown Books

ALSO BY CHAPELTOWN BOOKS

Theme and Variations
by Vanessa Horn

Theme and Variations is a collection of sixteen flash fiction stories with music – some of it harmonious, some discordant – running through them.

Although fictional, these stories also contain many elements of realism. After all, music will always be with, around or in you

Order from Amazon:

ISBN: 978-1-910542-51-4 (paperback)
978-1-910542-52-1 (ebook)

Chapeltown Books

140 x 140
by Gill James

This anthology of women's fiction, this collection of very short stories, some might say a flash collection, is thought-provoking and each story is based upon a tweet. Except that each piece is 140 words long and not 140 characters.

"In this entertaining book, Gill James chose the first picture she saw on her Twitter feed on specific dates. As the title suggests, there are 140 stories, each of 140 words. Some tales are laugh out loud funny, others thoughtful, and there are tragic stories too. Whatever your mood, you will find plenty to suit you here." *(Amazon)*

Order from Amazon:

ISBN: 978-1-910542-35-4 (paperback)
978-1-910542-36-1 (ebook)

Chapeltown Books